MY PUP ADVENTURE

This book was especially written for
Isaiah Hicks
with love from
The Purser's & Ashley

Based on the teleplay "Pups Pit Crew" by Franklin Young

Adapted by Kate Andresen

ISBN 978-1-875676-66-8

S0-AJU-841

Whenever there's trouble in Adventure Bay, the PAW Patrol save the day! They're six clever pups with special talents, ready to race to the rescue with their awesome vehicles and gadgets.

When Ryder calls, the PAW Patrol reports to the Lookout to get their rescue mission.

No job is too big, and no pup is too small!

Isaiah Hicks lives in Port Townsend, not far from Adventure Bay. Today is February 20th, Isaiah's birthday, and he, Caleb, Dakota and Sawyer are going to see their friend, Ryder.

Ryder takes Isaiah, Caleb, Dakota and Sawyer to the Lookout to meet the pups.

The pups line up.

"This is Chase," says Ryder. "He's our police pup. He can direct traffic, block off dangerous roads, or control a crowd. His super-sniffing nose can solve any mystery!"

"Chase drives a police truck. In his Pup Pack are a megaphone, a searchlight, a net, and other things to help keep the peace," says Ryder.

"Chase is on the case!" barks Chase.

"Marshall is our fire pup," says Ryder, introducing the Dalmatian to Isaiah, Caleb, Dakota and Sawyer. "He can be a little clumsy, but he's always ready to race to the rescue!"

"Marshall drives a fire truck. His Pup Pack holds a hose that helps him put out all kinds of trouble," Ryder tells his friends.

"I'm all fired up!" says Marshall.

"This is Rubble," he says next. "He's our construction pup. He loves to build and dig. He's also a great skateboarder and snowboarder!" says Ryder.

"Rubble has a digger with a bucket shovel and a drill. His Pup Pack opens into a scoop so he can dig into anything," explains Ryder.

"Let's dig it!" barks Rubble.

Next in line is Skye. "Skye is fearless, a flying daredevil," says Ryder. "She's the smallest on the team, but she's also the fastest! She's a great dancer, too!"

"Skye is amazing!" says Isaiah.

"Skye flies a helicopter and her Pup Pack has wings that pop out."

"This pup's gotta fly!" says Skye.

"This is Rocky," Ryder says. "He's our recycling pup. He's full of ideas and loves to turn someone else's trash into his treasure! He hates to get wet, so he can look a little scruffy sometimes," says Ryder.

"Rocky drives a recycling truck. His Pup Pack has lots of different tools and an awesome mechanical claw," says Ryder.

"Rocky to the rescue!" barks Rocky.

"And this is Zuma," Ryder says. "He's our water-rescue dog. He's always happy and full of energy. He loves the beach, surfing and diving!"

"He drives a hovercraft and his Pup Pack holds air tanks and propellers to help him dive deep underwater."

"Ready to dive in!" woofs Zuma.

"Sounds like a great team!" says Isaiah.

Meanwhile, outside Mr. Porter's café, Alex has just finished building a Super Trike from old parts he'd found.

"Hey grandpa," says Alex. "Check out what I made!"

"Nice!" says Mr. Porter. "And you used lots of duct tape."

"Just like you taught me," replies Alex.

Alex had also heard that Ryder has some visitors. Isaiah Hicks from Port Townsend was visiting, together with Caleb, Dakota and Sawyer.

Alex wants to ride over to show them his new Super Trike.

Alex puts on his helmet and tightens the strap.

He gives the trike a running push, hops on and pedals at full speed.

"Whoo-hoo!" he yells.

But the trike trips over the curb and falls apart! The parts roll everywhere.

"My Super Trike!" cries Alex.

"I was so looking forward to showing it to Ryder, Isaiah, Caleb, Dakota and Sawyer—but now I can't!"

Luckily, Mr. Porter has an idea. He takes out his phone and calls Ryder.

"I have an emergency...Alex could use some help with his Super Trike. I know you're pretty handy with vehicles!"

"Tell him we're on our way. PAW Patrol is on a roll!" cried Ryder.

Ryder calls the pups to the Lookout and explains the mission.

"Isaiah, Caleb, Dakota, Sawyer! Sounds like we may need your help, too!" says Ryder.

Isaiah hops on the back of Ryder's ATV. Chase, Rocky and Skye follow behind with Caleb, Dakota and Sawyer.

"Chase, I'll need you to stop traffic so we can safely find the parts of Alex's trike," says Ryder.

"Chase is on the case," replies Chase.

He directs traffic while Ryder and Alex pick up the parts.

Rocky brings the parts to the garage at the Lookout.

"Can you fix it?" asks Alex.

"Sure we can!" says Ryder.

Rocky and Ryder put the trike back together, only this time, it's much stronger!

"Awesome! Now my Super Trike can go extra, super fast!" says Alex. He was ready to speed off, but Ryder told him to wait.

"First you need to get used to your new vehicle. Let's take it for a slow drive down the Lookout Driveway."

"Isaiah, would you like to join us?" Ryder asks.

But Alex is so excited, he doesn't hear Ryder, and zooms off!

"Look at me go!" shouts Alex. But as he takes his feet off the pedals, they turn faster and faster and he skids around a tight bend. "This is too fast!" he cries. "Help!"

Isaiah, Caleb, Dakota, Sawyer and the pups race after him. He's headed for a busy street!

"Chase, secure the traffic at the bottom of the drive!" yells Ryder.

"Chase is on the case!" barks Chase.

Chase stops the traffic just as Alex zooms onto a bridge, followed closely by Ryder and Isaiah.

"Don't worry, Alex – the PAW Patrol is on it!" shouts Ryder.

"Skye," Ryder calls into his helmet microphone.
"I need you and your 'copter at the bridge!"

Skye flies her helicopter over the bridge.

"Can you hook Alex's trike?" Ryder asks.

"You got it, Ryder!" replies Skye.

She spots Alex and hooks onto his trike.

Isaiah cheers.

The trike stops! Alex is safe. He cheers and waves.

"Great flying, Skye!" shouts Isaiah.

"I'm sorry, Ryder," says Alex. "I just couldn't stop it. The trike was too super."

"That's okay, Alex," says Ryder. "But when you try something new, you have to start out easy."

Alex nods and smiles. "Thank you, PAW Patrol."

"And thank you, Isaiah, Caleb, Dakota and Sawyer," says Alex.

"Mission accomplished!" says Isaiah.

"You were such good pups today. How about we head to the ice cream stand?" says Ryder.

"Yeah! Let's race on over," says Alex.

Chase shakes his head. "Uh-uh," he says.

"I mean, roll on over," says Alex.

"Let's go!" says Ryder, taking the lead.
They all show Alex how to ride safely.

"You've earned the PAW Patrol Safe Driving Cup," says Ryder, handing Alex a trophy filled with ice cream.

"Yay!" says Alex.

Ryder turns to Isaiah, "Happy birthday, Isaiah. Thank you for sharing your special day with the PAW Patrol. Please come and visit us again soon."

Then the PAW Patrol all sing Happy Birthday to Isaiah!

This personalized PAW Patrol: My Pup Adventure book was especially created for Isaiah Hicks of 2364 Highland Loop, Port Townsend, with love from The Purser's & Ashley.

If Isaiah loved starring in this personalized My Adventure Book then there are many more exciting stories in our collection.

Simply visit us at www.identitydirect.com to create Isaiah's next adventure!

Alternatively, you can contact us by email at inquiry@identitydirect.com.

Lots of exciting titles to collect!